THE ADVENTU
SARAH AND THEODORE BODGITT

Pamela Oldfield

# The adventures of Sarah and Theodore Bodgitt

*Illustrated by Carolyn Dinan*

BROCKHAMPTON PRESS

*For Nicholas*
*and St John's Primary School, Sevenoaks*

ISBN 0 340 18327 6

First edition 1974
Published by Brockhampton Press Ltd,
Salisbury Road, Leicester
Printed in Great Britain by
Hazell Watson & Viney Ltd, Aylesbury, Bucks
Text copyright © 1974 Pamela Oldfield
Illustrations copyright © 1974 Brockhampton Press Ltd

3364
14. 2. 75

# Contents

# The rocking chair

Theodore Bodgitt was a giant of a man, with a bushy ginger beard. Everyone agreed that he was a nice old man but they also agreed that he was the laziest, most foolish man for miles around. He lived in a tumbledown farmhouse on a tumbledown farm which was hardly a farm any more, for the number of animals had dwindled over the years until a pig, a hen and a horse were all that remained. The plough stood rusting in the shed and the only land that was tilled was a small vegetable garden near the house.

But Theodore Bodgitt was quite unconcerned. He liked the farm as it was. He thought it just right and would sit in his favourite armchair, puffing at his pipe, at peace with the world. But if Theodore was at peace with the world his wife Sarah was not! At least, she may have been at peace with the world but she was not at peace with her lazy husband.

'Stir your stumps, you lazy good-for-nothing!' she would cry, in a voice that rattled the china on the shelf. 'The fence needs mending, the horse needs grooming, and you sit there puffing away at that pipe as though you haven't a care in the world. Get to your feet, Theodore Bodgitt and find some work to do or I'll box your ears for you!'

And Theodore was quite sure she would, for although she was only half his size she had a fiery temper, a well-sharpened tongue and was afraid of nothing and nobody.

One day when she had bullied him into cleaning out the pig's sty she put on her best bonnet and shawl and went off to the village to attend an auction. She dearly loved the excitement of a sale and always bought something however small. Once it was a brass bell and once a pair of bellows.

Today, however, she had set her heart on a rocking chair. It was brown polished wood with a red velvet seat and padded red velvet arms. Underneath, the rockers were held in place by metal springs and there were castors at the corners. Sarah sat down in the front row and waited for the bidding to start. At last Mr Biddle the auctioneer raised his mallet and pointed to the chair.

'Ladies and gentlemen, we have here a fine old rocking chair, in excellent condition. How much am I bid? Shall we say one pound?'

Sarah raised her hand, Mr Biddle nodded.

'One pound I am bid,' he said. 'Any advance on one pound?'

A young man behind Sarah raised his hand.

'Two pounds,' he said.

Sarah glared at him and took a quick peep inside her purse.

'Three pounds,' she cried and waited breathlessly.

Mr Biddle looked at the young man but he shook his head.

'Gone to Sarah Bodgitt for three pounds,' said Mr Biddle and Sarah clapped her hands with delight. She paid the money and hurried home. There she found her lazy husband leaning on the fork, half asleep.

'Theodore Bodgitt, what do you think you're doing?' she cried, bustling into the yard. 'You're dozing, you lazy old rascal, and the sty's as dirty as ever it was. Give me that fork. I shall have to do the job myself. You take yourself down to the auction room and fetch home the rocking chair with the red velvet seat. And take great care of it for it has cost me three pounds. Now look lively or you will feel the prongs of this fork!'

So saying she shooed him off and set to with a will to clean out the sty.

Theodore Bodgitt ambled along the lane and dawdled up the hill and finally arrived at the auction room just as they were closing. He soon found the chair and began to consider how best to get it home.

'I reckon I could carry it,' he said to himself, so he hoisted it onto his back and started off along the lane. But the chair was heavier than he thought and he soon grew tired. He set the chair down again and looked at it from all angles.

'Bless me if I couldn't scoot it home!' he cried, noticing the castors for the first time. He put one foot on the front, held onto the arms and pushed with his other foot. The rocking chair rolled along at a great pace but it would not go straight. It skittered wildly from side to side, dragging Theodore with it. Finally he ended up in the ditch. Grumbling and cursing he righted the chair and sat in it.

'Dratted old chair!' he muttered crossly, mopping his face with a handkerchief. 'It's more trouble than it's worth.'

Suddenly he realised that he was sitting in the chair near the top of the hill. A gleam came into his eye as he saw an easy way out of his troubles.

'I'll ride home,' he told himself. 'No need to wear myself out pushing and pulling. I'll let the chair do all the work. I'll just sit back and enjoy the ride. Theodore Bodgitt, you're a bright lad and no mistake.'

And before he could contradict himself he edged the chair to the top of the hill and prepared for a graceful descent into the farm yard. But he had badly underestimated the slope of the hill. The chair gathered speed at an alarming rate and fairly flew down the hill, scattering dust and stones in all directions.

'Help!' cried Theodore, clinging onto the chair for dear life. 'Help! Save me! I shall be airborne in a minute.'

Faster and faster the chair swooped down on the unsuspecting farm. Theodore closed his eyes and wished he had lived a better life. Suddenly there was a jolt as the chair reached the hedge and Theodore was thrown up into the air. He sailed over the hedge into the farm yard

and landed on the pile of straw which Sarah had raked out of the sty. He lay on his back with his legs in the air and groaned. Sarah turned and stared in surprise at her husband.

'Theodore Bodgitt!' she cried. 'Are you alive or dead? Tell me at once.'

'I'm alive, dearest wife,' he whispered. 'I'm alive.'

'Then stop lazing about in that straw,' said Sarah, 'and fetch my chair.'

Carefully Theodore picked himself up and felt himself all over.

'All in one piece, thank goodness,' he muttered and stumbled away to find the rocking chair.

But the chair, when he found it, was *not* in one piece. It had broken up when it hit the hedge and now lay in pieces well hidden in the long grass. Horrified Theodore fell to his knees and began to scrabble among the grass.

'Oh dear, oh dear,' he whispered. 'Sarah's not going to like this. She's not going to like it at all.'

At last he thought that he had found all the pieces. Clutching them awkwardly he wondered what to do next. Suddenly he had an idea. He hurried to the barn and locked himself in.

'I shall have to mend the dratted thing,' he

told himself gloomily, 'and a fine old job that will be. But mend it I must or my life won't be worth living.'

He spread the pieces round him on the floor and began to fit them together. It was ten times harder than the hardest jigsaw puzzle and Theodore had never been good at puzzles. He thought he had never worked so hard in his life but at last he was satisfied and reached for his pot of quick-drying glue. He was sticking one of the arms back onto the frame when Sarah's voice outside the barn made him jump guiltily.

'Theodore Bodgitt!' she cried. 'Why have you locked yourself in the barn? You are up to some mischief I'll be bound.'

'Mischief? No, no wife. Certainly not,' he stammered. 'I'm – er – I'm polishing your chair for you – for a surprise.'

'Polishing my chair?' cried Sarah in astonishment. 'That's not a surprise, Theodore, that's a shock and no mistake. Wonders will never cease!' And she was so touched she hurried away to the kitchen to make his favourite cake for supper.

Meanwhile poor Theodore had made a terrible discovery. The rocking chair was as good as new – except that one castor was missing.

'Bust my braces!' he said, greatly despairing, and rushed out to search again among the tall tussocky grass by the hedge. The sun dipped low in the sky and Theodore began to think he would end his search by moonlight but suddenly, there was the castor tucked under the hedge root.

He snatched it up and hurried back to the barn. He screwed it into place and stood back to admire his handiwork.

'Theodore Bodgitt, you're a genius,' he told himself, 'and no two ways about it.'

He polished the chair hastily and carried it proudly into the kitchen.

'There you are,' he said to his wife. 'What do you think of that? Aren't I a good husband?'

She glanced at the chair.

'What a fuss over a bit of polish!' she thought to herself but she said nothing. Instead she smiled at him, tugged his beard playfully and cut him a large slice of cake.

# The hidden money

When Theodore Bodgitt saw the pink envelope with the green writing on it, he groaned. Only one person wrote letters like that and that was Sarah's sister Matilda. And she only wrote such letters when she intended to pay them a visit.

'Well, isn't that nice,' said Sarah as she finished reading it. 'Matilda is coming to stay for a few days. I haven't seen her for such a long time. We'll have a great deal to talk about.'

'Talk is the word!' said Theodore. 'Your sister Matilda could talk the hind legs off a donkey! She chatters on and on until my head is spinning – and she always sits in my favourite chair. I don't want her to come!'

'Theodore Bodgitt! How can you say such terrible things?' cried Sarah. 'My only sister!

The only person I have left in the whole world!'

'You've got me, dearest,' said Theodore mildly.

'And a fat lot of good you are!' snapped Sarah. 'Look at you – still sitting over your dinner at half past one. There's the hedge to cut, the pig to feed, the gate to mend, the—'

'I'm going! I'm going!' cried her husband jumping to his feet, and he removed himself from the kitchen before she could think of any more jobs for him to do.

Sarah looked round the shabby kitchen and sighed. She felt ashamed of their tumbledown farmhouse. The curtains were old and hung limp and pale. The mats on the floor were faded and frayed. The cups and saucers were cracked and chipped and sadly at odds with each other. She sighed again and shook her head. Then, suddenly she straightened her back, tucked in a stray wisp of hair and marched out to find her husband.

'Theodore Bodgitt, the time has come for a

few changes,' she declared. 'I'm ashamed to let my sister see this shabby old place. You must give me some money and I'll go into town this very afternoon and—'

'Dearest!' said Theodore. 'Do think before you speak! I have no money for such luxuries. I am only a poor farmer.'

'If you're poor it's because you're so idle!' said Sarah angrily. 'You're a sly one, Theodore. I'm sure you've got some money hidden away somewhere because whenever I ask you for any you say you are saving for a rainy day. Surely you can spare a few pounds to brighten up the kitchen before your sister-in-law comes.'

But he just shook his head.

'If I had any money I would give it to you with pleasure,' he said, 'but I have none to give.'

'I see,' said Sarah grimly, and she turned on her heel and marched back into the house.

'Cunning old fox!' she grumbled. 'We'll see if there's any money or not. I'll search this house from top to bottom. He shan't get the better of me if I can help it.'

So saying she began to roam the house looking for likely hiding places. She looked everywhere. On top of the cupboards, under the stairs, down in the cellar and up in the attic. She prodded the mattress, shook every cushion and even poked her fingers into the toes of Theodore's Sunday boots but all to no purpose. She found nothing – not even a halfpenny. But at last, when it seemed there was nowhere else to look, the hands of the clock reached two o'clock and out popped the cuckoo.

'Cuckoo! Cuckoo!'

Sarah drew in her breath sharply.

'It's a cuckoo I am and no mistake,' she said, 'not to think of that before!'

Sure enough, in the back of the clock she found a small bundle of pound notes.

'Oh, the wily old skinflint!' she cried. 'But he did say he had nothing hidden away so this can't be his money! And if it's not his, why,

then it must be mine, for there's none but the two of us living here!'

She tucked the money into her purse and went into town, where she made several exciting purchases.

'Deliver them to the farm in the morning,' she told the shopkeeper, who agreed readily. It wasn't often he had such a good customer.

Next morning Theodore woke before his wife. He tossed and turned uneasily for some time, worrying about his hoard of money.

'I wonder if it's safe in that clock?' he thought. 'Perhaps I should move it. A burglar could easily find it. I'll take it up into the attic. It will be safer there.'

He heaved himself out of bed and padded downstairs in his bare feet. He put his hand into the back of the clock – and found nothing! For a moment he stood rooted to the spot. He turned white with fear, then red with rage!

'Thieves! Robbers! Burglars!' he bellowed. 'I've been robbed! Oh what wickedness! Oh what villainy! They shan't get away with it!'

Still in his nightshirt, he snatched up his shotgun and ran out into the yard, bellowing and cursing with all his might. From the bedroom window, his wife watched him go.

'Theodore Bodgitt, you're a silly old man!' she said. 'Oh well, no doubt the exercise will do you good. I can't stand about here watching you make a fool of yourself. Matilda is coming and I've a pie to bake and other matters to attend to.'

Promptly at ten o'clock Matilda arrived at the station. Sarah met her with the horse and cart and drove her home in triumph. They were cosily installed in the kitchen, and gossiping away to their hearts' content when Theodore burst in, panting and dishevelled. He looked round the kitchen – and then looked again. New curtains fluttered at the windows and a large fluffy rug covered the floor. Sarah wore a dress of soft red velvet and the two sisters were sipping their tea from new, blue cups!

'You must excuse Theodore's night shirt,' said Sarah, 'but he ran out after a fox. Did you shoot it, dearest?'

Theodore didn't answer. New curtains? A new rug? He was beginning to understand what had happened to his money. Sarah had found it!

Matilda smiled at him.

'What a generous man you are, Theodore,' she said, 'to buy all these new things for Sarah! She has just been telling me. I wish my husband was like you. I've been telling Sarah, she is a very fortunate woman!'

He looked at his wife and she smiled sweetly at him. He opened his mouth and then closed it again. There really wasn't anything to be said. Slowly he went upstairs to dress.

'If I live to be a hundred,' he said to himself, 'I shall *never* understand that wife of mine!'

# Grunter the pig

The pig looked at Theodore and Theodore looked at the pig.

'Time you were bacon!' said Theodore sternly. 'You're getting so fat you'll burst one of these days. Look at you – gobbling away there. You ought to be ashamed of yourself!'

But Grunter, the pig, was *not* ashamed of himself. Not one bit of it! He was a very happy pig. He had lived with Sarah and Theodore ever since he was a piglet and life was good. He had a sty to live in, three good meals a day and Sarah to scratch his back for him whenever she had time. He gave Theodore a scornful glance and carried on with his breakfast.

'Time that pig was killed,' said Theodore to his wife, as she washed up the breakfast things.

'He'll make fine bacon and good pork chops, not to mention sausages! I'll take him down to the butcher's later on today.'

But Sarah had turned from the sink and was staring at him.

'Kill the pig?' she said in astonishment. 'Kill dear old Grunter? You must be mad, Theodore Bodgitt! You'll do no such thing!'

'But dearest,' sighed Theodore. 'Why have we raised him, if not for bacon and chops? Why have we fed him all these months, and why have I cleaned his sty out time after time? And what is going to become of him if we don't eat him?'

'We are not going to eat that pig!' said Sarah stubbornly. 'Why, we've had him ever since he was a baby. He was such a cute little fellow. Do you remember how he used to run out of his sty to greet me. He knew the sound of my voice. Oh Theodore, how could you even think of killing him? You wicked man!'

And she hid her face in her apron and sobbed loudly. Theodore felt very uncomfortable,

because he hated to see his wife so unhappy. He patted her shoulder gently.

'There, there, don't cry,' he said kindly. 'We won't kill him if you say not, but we really cannot afford to keep him any longer. Supposing I take him to the market and sell him, then buy another animal. If I buy a sheep we can sell the wool and we won't need to eat the sheep. A sheep is much more use than a pig. Now, what do you say to that idea?'

Sarah dried her tears and declared it a splendid idea. She set to work with a will to make Grunter presentable. She washed him with scented soap, polished his hooves with floor polish, and brushed his bristles with the shoe brush. Then she gave him a push up into the cart and waved them 'goodbye' with a cheery smile.

'Well,' said Theodore to himself, as they bowled along the lane. 'I'm a clever man, though I say it as shouldn't. I can twist that wife of mine round my little finger! We shall be well rid of this useless animal. A sturdy sheep will be much more profitable.'

He was still thinking along these lines when he arrived back at the farm with a large woolly sheep in the cart behind him. Sarah ran out of the house, greatly excited.

'Theodore Bodgitt!' she cried. 'You certainly are a fine judge of animals. It's a very fine sheep! A very fine sheep indeed. Look at the length of the fleece! That will be worth a pretty penny! And it is so intelligent. See the expression on its face! I do believe it knows what we are saying.'

They lifted it down from the cart and admired it.

'It won't even need a shed,' said Theodore craftily. 'Sheep are used to being out in all weathers. They don't need coddling like a pig.'

'You're right, husband,' said Sarah. 'All this sheep needs is plenty of rich grass to eat. Not the scrubby, scrawny stuff that grows around here, but the long, lush grass that grows on the hillside.' And she pointed to the mountains that towered behind the farm. 'Every morning you must rise at dawn and take the sheep up the hillside to find the best grass. Don't worry about the little jobs around the farm. I'll do them. Your job will be to spend all day on the hillside with this fine sheep.'

'*All* day!' stammered Theodore. 'But what about my dinner? I'll have to come home for my dinner.'

'No need to bother with dinner,' said Sarah firmly. 'I'll cut you some sandwiches. And think of all the exercise you will be getting – and all that fresh air. Of course, it won't be so pleasant in the winter but you'll soon get used to it.'

But Theodore was not so sure! He had no intention of missing his dinner every day for the sake of a sheep, however fine, and he did not see himself as a mountaineer. Without another word he bundled the sheep back into the cart and set off once more for the market. He was soon back with a goat and Sarah was at the door to greet him.

'Theodore Bodgitt,' she cried. 'You've bought a goat! You are a clever man. You must have known I've always wanted a goat!'

'It's a nanny goat, you see,' said her husband proudly. 'It will give milk and yet it won't eat as much as a cow.'

'How sensible you are!' said Sarah lovingly. 'You see things so clearly. Tomorrow you must go to town and buy a stool to sit on, and a pail. You must milk it every morning and evening – and you must make it a good, strong shed. Goats can't abide draughts, you know. Then you must make it a run so it does not wander away. A run with a good, high fence. Goats can jump, you know – why, Theodore! You are putting it back into the cart! Have you changed your mind again?'

Theodore went back to town in a fair temper.

'That wife of mine is the very devil!' he grumbled. 'Whatever I bring home she will find some way of making me work harder than I did before. But I think I can be cleverer!'

Sarah was pegging out the washing when Theodore drove, puffing and clanking, into the yard. She was so surprised she dropped his clean shirt into a muddy puddle and nearly swallowed the peg she was holding in her mouth.

'Theodore Bodgitt, am I seeing things?' she cried.

'No dearest,' said her husband grimly. 'This is a car! I sold the goat *and* the horse *and* the cart to buy it. Now aren't you going to tell me how clever I am?'

'But why do we need a car?' said Sarah. 'It doesn't give milk and it has no fleece. The horse and cart were fast enough for our needs. I don't like these new-fangled contraptions!'

'But *I* do,' said Theodore,' and I'll tell you why. It doesn't eat anything, and I shan't have to make it a run! I shan't have to milk it, and I shan't have to take it up the mountains looking for grass!'

Sarah looked at her husband and she looked at the car. At last she smiled.

'I'm a silly old woman!' she said simply. 'Of course you are right, dearest. This car is a splendid buy, and you are a clever man. With a car we shall be able to visit Matilda in Scotland. Won't she be surprised? And we can visit great-aunt Doris in Ireland and your Uncle Willie in Wales! Oh, I can hardly wait to be on our way. I must see what I have that's fit to wear.'

And she darted back into the house and ran up the stairs to the bedroom. But she didn't go to the wardrobe. She peeped out of the window instead to see what her husband was doing. As she expected he was driving the car back along the lane. Sarah sat on the bed and laughed.

'And when he comes back he'll be driving the horse and cart,' she said gleefully, 'and dear old Grunter will be with him, or my name's not Sarah Bodgitt.'

And, of course, her name *was* Sarah Bodgitt and Grunter was soon back in his sty eating a big supper.

# Theodore's diet

Sarah Bodgitt looked at her husband one morning and frowned.

'Theodore!' she said. 'You are getting tubby. Definitely tubby. I might almost say fat. You eat too much and you don't work hard enough. That's your trouble.'

Theodore looked down at himself in pained surprise.

'Fat?' he said. 'Oh no, no! I'm well covered but I'm not fat.'

'You're fat,' insisted his wife. 'Look at you – you can hardly fasten that jacket. It's a diet for you, I'm thinking!'

Theodore turned pale at the word 'diet' and lowered himself into a chair.

'Not a diet,' he begged. 'It would kill me. You know how faint I get if I don't get enough to eat.'

'Nonsense!' cried Sarah. 'You can start to-day. I think an apple and a glass of water will do for your breakfast.'

He stared at her miserably.

'But I always have bacon and eggs,' he moaned, 'with a few tomatoes and a sausage—'

'Not today,' said Sarah firmly. 'Now eat up your apple and be quick about it. There's some wood to be chopped for the fire, and the exercise will do you good.'

And she bustled away upstairs and was soon shaking the rugs out of the window in a flurry of activity.

By dinner time a delicious stew was simmering on the stove. Theodore sniffed hungrily.

'What a good woman Sarah is,' he thought. 'She knows stew is one of my favourite dinners. Mmm! Lumps of tender meat and juicy carrots – not to mention the onions.'

Quite overcome by the thought of it, he lifted the lid. Then he stared into the pot. There was only enough stew for one helping!

'Why, Sarah,' he cried. 'Aren't you having any stew today? There is very little here.'

'I'm having some but you're not!' said Sarah. 'It's salad for you, my lad. Nice crisp lettuce and tomatoes. Now wash your hands and pull up a chair.'

'But why aren't you having salad?' wailed Theodore. 'It's not fair!'

'Me eat salad?' laughed Sarah. 'Just take a look at me – all skin and bone and as frail as a

bird! I need good, nourishing food, and plenty of it, before I disappear altogether! Do stop goggling like a frog and eat your salad.'

This awful state of affairs lasted for days and days. As Theodore grew thinner his moans grew louder until food was all he could think about. He planned to slip into the cake shop as soon as he could get into town, but Sarah kept him so busy there was no time. At last, after a whole week of dieting he declared himself too weak to get out of bed.

'I am too weak to move!' he told Sarah, in a feeble voice. 'I shall lie here and die of starvation. You will be rid of me at last!'

'No such luck!' said his wife tartly. 'You'll be out of that bed in two seconds or I'll pull you out!'

'Oh you wicked woman!' cried Theodore, throwing off the bedclothes. 'And what is that delicious smell coming from the kitchen?'

'Porridge for my breakfast,' said Sarah, and she flew down the stairs to catch it before it burnt.

Theodore groaned and shook his head despairingly. 'Lovely thick creamy porridge with sugar on it!' he whispered. 'Oh what is to become of me?'

There was no one to answer his question so he sighed deeply and stumbled downstairs to eat his apple. He was a very unhappy man.

Later that day he chanced to see Sarah at work in the vegetable patch.

'Now, what is she planting?' he said curiously, and went a little nearer. 'Can it be—? Yes, I believe it is! It's onions! Round, golden onions! Mmm!'

He went nearer still and his wife glanced up. Theodore smiled hopefully at her.

'Those onions look very good, wife,' he said. 'There's nothing better than a dish of onions with a rich, white sauce!'

'They're not onions,' said Sarah, 'and do try to stop thinking about food. I thought you were going to mend the stable door this afternoon and here you are still drifting about like a ship without an anchor.'

Theodore knew when he was beaten. He found some screws and a screwdriver and set to to strengthen the hinges on the stable-door. But he didn't stop thinking about food. Not a bit of it! He thought about the onions all the afternoon, all the evening, and well into the night. He lay awake imagining the onions steaming on a plate; he imagined how they would taste, and how delightfully full he would feel after he had eaten them. Finally, when he could bear it no longer, he got out of bed and crept downstairs. Out into the moon-lit garden he went – straight to the vegetable patch. Frantically he dug and dug into the soft earth with his bare hands.

'One . . . two . . . three . . .' He pulled the onions out of the ground and piled them neatly. 'Six . . . seven . . . eight . . .' Soon he had them all. He took them into the kitchen and put them on to boil. While they boiled he did his best to make a white sauce. At last it was ready to eat. Theodore took a deep breath and put the first forkful into his mouth.

'Mmm! Delicious!' he murmured happily
and in went a second mouthful. 'Not a very
strong flavour, these onions – but very good!'

He ate and ate until the plate was empty,
then he lay back in the chair feeling content
for the first time for a week. He was so full
it was all he could do to get up and wash
the pans, but he daren't leave them for
Sarah to find in the morning. When the
kitchen was tidy once more he went back

to bed and slept peacefully until the morning.

He woke to find his wife shaking him by the arm.

'Wake up, lazy bones!' she laughed. 'Are you planning to sleep all day as well as all night? I've got a nice surprise for you, Theodore. Today we are going to have roast beef, Yorkshire pudding, peas and roast potatoes! Your diet is over. I think you are slim enough. Now, what do you think of that?'

'I think you are the sweetest woman in the world!' said Theodore. 'Roast beef will be very acceptable, I assure you.'

'Well, stir yourself,' said Sarah,' and chop some wood for the stove. I'll be back from town within the hour. I have to buy some more daffodil bulbs while I'm there. All the ones I planted yesterday have disappeared. I think the mice must have eaten them.'

'Daffodil bulbs!' cried Theodore. 'Surely you mean onions?'

'No, I don't,' said Sarah. 'They were daffodil bulbs I planted. I thought we could sell some flowers in the market next spring. Well, I'll be off.'

Theodore watched her go, with wildly rolling eyes.

'Daffodil bulbs!' he moaned. 'I'm poisoned! Why, oh why, am I such a greedy, foolish old man? And today we are having roast beef! – I feel so ill I don't think I shall be able to eat a single mouthful! Still, this has taught me a lesson. From now on I shall be a reformed character!'

But, needless to say, he wasn't!

# The little dog

Wednesday was market day. Although Theodore had no animals to sell, having only a hen, a pig and a horse, he often went to the market, just to meet his friends. One day as they all stood inspecting the calves Theodore made a startling discovery. He was the only farmer without a dog! Farmer Toogood had a black and white collie. Farmer Bennett had a golden labrador. Farmer Sweet had a sad looking spaniel, and even Farmer Grundy had a perky little mongrel. Only Theodore was without a dog! He walked home from the market feeling very sorry for himself.

'What is the matter,' said Sarah, when she saw the expression on his face. 'You look about as happy as a fish in the desert! Are you sick?'

'No,' said Theodore.

'Have you lost something?'

'No,' he said again.

'Have you had an argument with one of your friends?'

'No, no, no!'

'Then I shall stop guessing, Theodore Bodgitt,' said Sarah, 'and you shall tell me, for you'll have no peace until you do!'

Theodore took a deep breath and faced his wife.

'I want a dog,' he said.

Sarah's eyes widened in astonishment.

'A dog?' she cried. 'A dog? A nasty, noisy dog? Why, Theodore Bodgitt, whatever can you want with a dog? Troublesome things, they are. In and out of the house with muddy feet! Barking and growling at everyone – and biting the postman as like as not! Not to mention eating us out of house and home! Really Theodore, you do get some funny ideas into your head!'

'But Sarah,' protested her husband,' every farmer needs a dog to round up the sheep!'

'But you haven't got any sheep,' said his wife.

'Well then, to bring in the cows at milking time.'

'You haven't got any cows.'

'Why then, to keep away burglars.'

'Theodore Bodgitt, you know very well we have nothing worth stealing. We do *not* need a dog!'

Poor Theodore gave up. He knew it was no good arguing with his wife. He said no more about it, and Sarah thought he had given up the idea, but the very next time he went to the market, the first thing he saw was a litter of puppies for sale!

He stood watching the five little puppies as they wriggled and snuffled in a cardboard box.

'Nice little dogs, they are,' said their owner persuasively. 'Father was a mongrel but their mother was a labrador. They're sturdy little dogs. You looking for a dog, sir?'

'No,' said Theodore. 'At least – I am and I'm not – that is – yes!'

The man put one of the puppies into Theo-dore's arms and the little dog snuggled down into the warmth of his jacket.

'He likes you!' said the man. 'Taken a fancy to you, he has. Would you believe it!'

Theodore made up his mind. He paid the man, tucked the puppy into his jacket, and set off for home. But on the way his courage failed.

'You see, my wife doesn't like dogs,' he told

the puppy. 'She'll make me take you back to the market. I think I'll hide you in the barn for a few days until I can catch her in a good mood.'

So the puppy was hidden away in a dark corner of the barn. Theodore lined a box with warm cloth and managed to smuggle some food out to him. The puppy was very good until it grew dark and then he began to howl.

'Listen!' cried Sarah. 'Do you hear that noise? It sounds like a dog howling.'

'I don't hear anything,' said Theodore innocently. 'Perhaps it is an owl hooting.'

The next night the puppy began to bark.

'Listen!' cried Sarah.' Do you hear that noise? It sounds like a dog barking.'

'I don't hear anything,' said Theodore. 'Perhaps it is a fox.'

The next night the puppy climbed out of his box and knocked over a pile of apple trays.

'Someone is in our barn!' cried Sarah nervously. 'Do go and have a look, husband.'

Theodore hurried out to the barn and put the puppy back into his box.

'There was no one there, dearest,' he told his wife. 'The horse had kicked over his manger. I expect he is feeling frisky tonight.'

But the following night the puppy got out of the barn and scratched at the kitchen door. No one heard him because Sarah and Theodore were both asleep in bed, but the next morning they found scratches on the door.

'Whatever has been scratching at the door?' said Sarah.

'I don't know,' said Theodore. 'It may have been a badger. They get very bold when they're hungry.'

Now this state of affairs might have gone on for a very long time, but it so happened that

Sarah's friend Hannah Sweet came to call. The two ladies sat drinking their tea and talking about this and that. Suddenly Sarah remembered the strange noises she had been hearing and the strange scratches on the door. She told her friend about them.

'Come and see the scratches for yourself,' she said and led the way to the back door. Hannah studied the scratches and frowned. Then she looked grim.

'These marks were not made by a badger, Sarah,' she said slowly. 'A badger's claws would make bigger marks. I think the marks were made by a rat!'

Sarah backed away from the door in horror.

'A rat?' she whispered. 'Oh no! Not a rat! I simply cannot abide rats! The very thought of a rat makes my legs turn to jelly! Oh dear, oh dear, I shall have to sit down.'

'There, there,' said Hannah soothingly. 'Don't upset yourself, my dear. I'll pour you another cup of tea and you'll soon feel better.'

'I should have guessed,' said Sarah. 'We have

no cats. A cat would keep away the rats. I will ask Theodore to buy a cat.'

'If you want my advice,' said Hannah, passing Sarah another cup of tea, 'you'll ask him to buy a dog. A dog is more a match for a rat than ever a cat could be. Rats can be very dangerous if they're cornered. What you need is a dog.'

Poor Sarah shuddered and sipped her tea hurriedly. She made up her mind to ask Theodore as soon as he came in, and she waited anxiously for his return.

Theodore, meanwhile, had come to an important decision. He had made up his mind to tell Sarah about the dog.

'Must I go on bended knee in my own house?' he asked himself angrily. 'Am I a man or a mouse? I shall show her the dog and I shall insist on keeping it. Nothing she can say will make me change my mind!'

So saying he went straight to the barn, took the puppy from his box, and marched into the kitchen. Sarah looked up and saw the puppy.

To Theodore's surprise she sprang to her feet, a smile lighting her face.

'Theodore!' she cried. 'Oh you darling, clever man! You've bought a dog!'

She ran forward and took the puppy in her arms.

'You sweet little pet,' she crooned, patting and stroking it lovingly. 'You dear little mite. Such a brave little fellow and such sharp little teeth! Husband, you were right and I was wrong – a dog is just what we need!'

# Sarah wants a holiday

The needles stopped clicking and Sarah put down her knitting.

'Do you know, Theodore,' she said. 'We have been married for thirty-five years. Thirty-five long years. Just think of that!'

'Yes, dear,' said Theodore, wondering what was coming next.

'Thirty-five years,' said Sarah, 'and we've never had a holiday. Just think of that!'

'Now Sarah, don't start nagging me about a holiday,' said her husband firmly. 'You know I don't hold with holidays. Foolish waste of time and money, if you ask me. I've never had a holiday in my life and I don't intend to start now.'

'But Theodore,' cried Sarah, 'how do you know that holidays are a waste of time and money if you've never had one? Matilda's husband takes her to the seaside every summer. Now wouldn't you like to go to the seaside, Theodore?'

'No!' said Theodore.

'But just imagine it,' said Sarah. 'Golden sands, the warm blue sea, and nothing to do all day except relax and enjoy yourself. We could go on the pier and walk in the park, and Matilda tells me they sell sticks of rock and funny hats! Oh Theodore, wouldn't it be fun?'

'No,' said Theodore sourly. 'It would *not* be fun! The sea would be cold, the rock would make my tooth ache and I never wear funny hats.'

Sarah threw her knitting to the floor and jumped to her feet.

'Theodore Bodgitt, you're a selfish old man!' she cried. 'You only think about yourself! Don't you think I deserve a holiday? I've worked hard for you for thirty-five years and I'm tired.'

'Worked hard?' said her husband in surprise. 'Tired? Why, Sarah, you know you have a very easy life. Nothing to do all day but a little cooking and cleaning. You should think yourself a very fortunate woman. Now I will hear no more about a holiday. The answer is "No".'

Poor Sarah threw her apron over her face and burst into tears. She sobbed and wailed and begged and pleaded but nothing, it seemed, would make her husband change his mind.

Next morning Sarah lay in bed beside her sleeping husband and began to groan. She groaned louder and louder and louder until at last she woke up her husband. Theodore looked at her in alarm.

'Why Sarah,' he said anxiously, 'whatever is the matter?'

'I don't rightly know,' said Sarah weakly. 'I ache all over and I have a pain in my leg. I think you had better fetch the doctor.'

'What now?' cried Theodore. 'But I haven't had any breakfast yet. Aren't you going to cook my breakfast?'

'I'm afraid not,' said Sarah, 'but you can do it. It won't take a moment.'

Theodore slid out of bed feeling very disgruntled. He washed and dressed and stumped down the stairs.

'Now then,' he grumbled, 'where is the bacon, I wonder, and where is the frying pan?'

He did not find them because he was a foolish man and he looked in all the wrong places. So at last he had to go back upstairs and ask Sarah. Then when he had them he discovered that cooking is not as easy as it looks. The egg was runny, the bacon burnt, and the tea, when he made it, was tepid.

'Drat it!' he said. 'I don't think I want any breakfast, after all. I've lost my appetite.' He went to the bottom of the stairs and called up to his wife.

'I'm just going to fetch the doctor.'

'Oh Theodore, do the washing up before you go,' cried Sarah. 'I should die of shame if the doctor saw my kitchen all at sixes and sevens!'

So Theodore washed up, and then set off for the doctor, who said he would come at once. He examined Sarah and then went downstairs to speak to Theodore who was waiting in the hall.

'Your wife is not at all well,' he said, 'but it is too early to say what is the matter. It may be that she is over-tired—'

'Over-tired?' said Theodore incredulously. 'Oh no doctor. I don't think so. You see, she has a very easy life – just a little cooking and cleaning, that's all. She can't possibly be over-tired.'

'Well, we shall see,' said the doctor, hiding a little smile. 'She must have a day in bed today and I will call again tomorrow. Goodbye to you, Farmer Bodgitt.'

As soon as the doctor had gone Theodore hurried into the larder to cut himself a slice of cheese because he had had no breakfast, but before he could eat it Sarah called him and he hurried upstairs.

'Would you tidy the bed for me, please,' she

57

said, 'and then make me a little porridge? The doctor said I must try to keep my strength up.'

He tidied the bed as best he could and went downstairs to make the porridge.

'Here you are, dearest,' he said, handing her a bowl of very lumpy porridge. 'Now I'm just going to sit down—'

'Sit down?' said Sarah. 'But you must chop some wood or the fire will go out – and don't forget to feed the hen, the pig and the horse. While you are doing that I will have a little sleep. It will do me good.'

She lay in bed listening to her husband bustling about below. The moment he had finished she called him once again.

'I've just remembered it's Monday,' she said, 'and Monday is washday. You'll find the soap under the sink. The dirty linen is in the basket and the pegs are on the windowsill. It's a fine blowy day so they will soon dry. While you are doing that I will be writing a shopping list for you to take into town.'

Poor Theodore stumbled downstairs speechlessly. How he longed to sit down and rest but there was no time. He washed the clothes and hung them on the line to dry. Then he took the shopping list, a bag and some money and went into town for the second time that day.

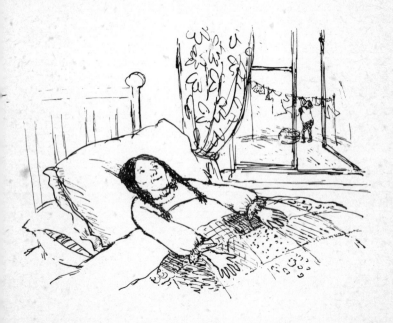

'Mrs Bodgitt ill, is she?' asked the butcher sympathetically. 'I am sorry to hear that. My wife was ill once, you know, for a whole week! My goodness me, I was glad to see her better. I had to do all the housework. I was quite worn out, I can tell you. Well, give her my kind regards. I hope she will soon be better.'

Theodore hoped so too. The thought that she, too, might be ill for a whole week sent shivers up and down his spine! Hurriedly he collected all the things on the list and took them home.

'Oh Theodore, how capable you are!' cried Sarah. 'And so quick. Now we can have an early dinner. First peel the potatoes and put them on to boil. Then wash and slice the beans. Prick the sausages and put them in the frying pan and make a little gravy. Quite a simple job, really. Wake me up when it's ready.'

And she turned over and pretended to go to sleep.

Theodore had a terrible time! The potatoes boiled over, hot fat splashed onto his hand and the gravy stuck to the saucepan and burnt. But Sarah declared it 'very tasty' and ate every bit!

After dinner Sarah asked for her knitting.

'I'm feeling a lot better,' she said brightly. 'Perhaps I shall be able to get up tomorrow.'

'I do hope so dearest,' said Theodore fervently. 'I really do hope so. I am quite worn out!'

'Worn out?' said Sarah in surprise. 'But you haven't been doing anything, have you? Just a little cooking and cleaning – and that reminds me. Bring in the washing, before it gets too dry to iron. You'll find the iron on the shelf by the window. Then there is only the floor to be scrubbed and a cake to bake for tea. I usually do a little polishing but perhaps you could do that after tea.'

In this way she managed to keep her husband busy all day. When he fell into bed that night he was exhausted! Next day, when the doctor called he was surprised to find Sarah up and about and as perky as ever.

'Good morning, doctor,' she said gaily. 'The rest in bed has done me good. I feel much better today. It is poor Theodore who is in bed. He is quite worn out after all that housework yesterday! But never mind. Tomorrow we are off to the seaside. Theodore has decided we need a holiday. Such a thoughtful man, Theodore Bodgitt!'

# Theodore mends the roof

Sarah and Theodore lay in bed one night listening to the storm that raged outside. The wind howled and flashes of lightning and claps of thunder kept them from their sleep.

'I do hope the horse is safe,' said Sarah anxiously. 'Last time we had a storm he kicked open his door and ran away!'

'I've mended the door,' said Theodore. 'He will be quite safe.'

'And the pig,' said Sarah. 'The drain in his sty was blocked up last time it rained and he was standing knee deep in water by the morning.'

'I've cleared that drain,' said her husband wearily. 'The pig will be quite safe.'

'What about the hen?' said Sarah. 'Last time

it was windy the lid of the dustbin was blown against the hen house! She got such a fright she didn't lay a single egg for a whole week.'

'I've moved the dustbins,' said Theodore. 'The hen will be quite safe. Do stop worrying, Sarah. We will *all* be quite safe,'

But that is where he was wrong. Above them, on the roof, a loose tile was suddenly lifted by the wind and went slithering down the roof to settle in the gutter. The rain discovered the small hole left by the tile and began to trickle through. Splash! A large drop of water fell onto Theodore's nose and he leaped out of bed.

'What was that?' he cried. 'Something fell on me! Something wet!'

'I can't see anything,' said his wife. 'I expect you imagined it. Do get back into bed or you will get a chill.'

Muttering, Theodore climbed back into bed but he had only been there for a few seconds when – Splash! A large drop of water fell right into his ear. He jumped out of bed and lit the lamp. On the ceiling, above the bed, was a large, wet patch.

'Theodore, the roof is leaking!' cried Sarah. 'I've been telling you for months there was a loose tile. Tomorrow you must fetch the builder.'

'Fetch the builder for that simple job!' he said scornfully. 'I can easily replace a loose tile. I'll do it first thing in the morning.'

After breakfast he went to the barn and took out his longest ladder. He carried it round to the front of the house. As soon as his head was level with the roof he saw the loose tile and carried it down to show his wife.

'See, here it is,' he told her. 'Now all I need is a hammer and a couple of nails. I'll have this tile back in place before you can say "Jack Robinson".' True to his word he had it back on the roof with a few sharp taps of the hammer. Sarah watched admiringly from the kitchen door.

'Well done!' she said. 'You are a much cleverer man than I ever thought you were.

You've – oh! Theodore! Do be careful!'

But it was too late. Somehow Theodore's foot slipped on the tiles and, like the tile the night before, he went slithering down the roof. Down, down and over the edge! Desperately he caught at the gutter and hung there, swinging to and fro.

'Quick, Sarah, do something!' he yelled. 'The gutter is going to break in a moment! Help!'

Terrified, Sarah rushed into the house and came out with her arms full of cushions which she threw onto the ground beneath Theodore's dangling feet. With a horrible 'Crack' the gutter broke away from the wall and Theodore crashed down onto the cushions, bringing the gutter with him.

'Theodore, are you hurt?' cried Sarah, struggling to help him to his feet.

'Of course I'm not hurt, woman, do stop fussing,' grumbled her husband. 'Just a little accident, that's all!'

'Then you had better go into town,' said his

wife, 'and fetch the builder to put that gutter back.'

'Certainly not!' said Theodore. '*I* shall put it back. It's quite a simple job. All it needs is a few nails in the right place.'

And to Sarah's dismay he went into the shed to look for some more nails.

'Mercy on us!' said Sarah. 'I simply dare not watch! I shall go into the kitchen and do the washing.'

Theodore climbed up the ladder once more and carefully nailed the gutter back into place. He went down again and was trying to move the ladder when it slipped sideways and the top end went straight through the bedroom window!

'Theodore Bodgitt! Whatever have you done now?' cried Sarah, rushing outside.

'Nothing, dearest,' said Theodore sheepishly. 'A small accident, that's all. I can soon put it right.'

'A small accident!' cried Sarah. 'Is that what you call it? *I* call it a big accident. You must go into town immediately and fetch the glazier.'

'No need to bother the glazier,' said Theodore airily. 'It's a simple thing to put in a pane of glass. I shall do it myself.'

Without a word Sarah returned to the kitchen. She sat down on the rocking chair, shut her eyes, and put her hands over her ears!

Meanwhile Theodore had found a piece of glass. He measured it and cut it to size. Up the ladder he went once more and had soon knocked out the old pane and set in the new. He pressed putty round the edges to hold it in place and went in search of some paint.

'A few dabs of paint will finish the job,' he told himself. 'Sarah is going to be very surprised when she sees it. She'll be sorry she has so little faith in me!'

Whistling happily he repainted the frame, and was about to descend when Sarah came out of the kitchen with a basket of newly-washed clothes.

'Look at the window now, Sarah,' called Theodore proudly. 'I told you it was a simple job! The glazier himself could have done no better!'

Sarah took no notice, but began to peg the clothes onto the line.

'Sarah!' called Theodore again. 'Do look at the window!'

She pegged up the last shirt and turned reluctantly, and inspected his handiwork.

'We-ell,' she said at last. 'You've certainly made a better job of it than I expected.'

Theodore smiled modestly.

'The loose tile is back on the roof! The gutter is as good as new, and the window frame has a new coat of paint!' he boasted. 'And all done by – WHOOPS!'

The paint pot slipped suddenly from his grip and fell to the ground below. Sarah screamed as bright blue paint splattered in all directions! It went over the kitchen window and over the kitchen door! It went up the wall and across the yard! It went over the clean clothes and, worst of all, it went over Sarah! She stood aghast as the drops of bright blue paint rained down. Seizing his chance, Theodore climbed nimbly down and took to his heels in the direction of the woods.

It took Sarah a moment or two to realise that he had gone, but when she did she gave a roar of rage that could be heard for miles around. Then she took a deep breath, snatched up the yard broom, and set off after him!

# Forty fine fat strawberries

'Those strawberries are nearly ripe,' said Sarah one morning. 'I have just counted forty fine fat strawberries. Maybe this year we shall be lucky enough to keep some for ourselves!'

Every year they planted two rows of strawberry plants and lavished a great deal of attention on them. They watered them when it was dry; pulled out every weed the moment it appeared, and laid straw under the young fruits to keep them clean. All to no avail! The moment the strawberries were ripe enough to eat – they disappeared! No one saw them go, but go they did.

'I'm blest if we'll lose them this year,' said Theodore. 'I'll find out what happens to them if it's the last thing I do!'

He decided to keep watch from the bedroom window. Before long three large, black crows flew down and began to hop among the plants. Theodore ran downstairs to Sarah.

'It's the crows!' he told her. 'The thieving rascals! I'll soon put a stop to that!'

He found an old hat, a jacket and an old pair of trousers and was soon at work, fashioning a scarecrow. The head he made from an old turnip with straw for hair. Then he put the hat on it and stuck it onto a pole. Another pole made the arms and on went the jacket. He stuffed the trousers with more straw and tied them onto the pole below the jacket.

'There!' he said proudly as Sarah inspected the finished scarecrow. 'That will scare away the crows – or I'm a Dutchman!'

Well, he wasn't a Dutchman and it did scare them. They took one look at it and fluttered away, squawking with fright. Theodore was well pleased with his morning's work but he was so tired from his efforts that as soon as he had finished his dinner he found a cosy spot under a hedge, and slept away the afternoon.

He didn't give the strawberries another thought. Imagine his feelings, then, when he went down the garden later that evening and found only thirty fine, fat strawberries!

'Something else has been eating them!' he told Sarah angrily. 'I shall keep another watch tomorrow and see what it is.'

So the next morning he settled down at the bedroom window and waited. At first he saw nothing but then his keen eyes picked out a tiny movement among the strawberry plants.

'It's mice!' he cried, jumping to his feet and he set off, without more ado, to buy three mouse traps. As soon as he got home he cut three cubes of cheese to bait the traps.

'We shall have no more trouble now, wife,' he said. 'There'll be no more disappearing strawberries, you mark my words!'

He carried the traps down the garden and hid them under the leaves of the strawberry plants. Within an hour he had caught three mice! He was so delighted with this success that he whistled and sang all the afternoon, until Sarah put her head out of the kitchen window.

'Whistling's a useless hobby!' she told him. 'Why not do something useful, like watering the strawberry plants. It has been a very hot day and we must make sure that the straw-berries are juicy ones.'

'Splendid idea,' said Theodore happily and he took the jug Sarah handed him and filled it at the pump. As he poured the water over the plants the thought crossed his mind that all was not well. He put down the jug and began to count – 'seventeen, eighteen, nineteen, twenty!'

'Only twenty?' he roared. 'Only twenty! After all my trouble something else has been eating them! Woe betide whatever it is!'

The next morning he was up at dawn, watching from the window. Suddenly four large wood-pigeons flew out from a nearby oak and began to strut among the strawberries, quite unperturbed by the scarecrow which flapped angrily at them. Theodore was so enraged he could hardly load his shotgun, but when he did – Bang! Bang! Bang! Bang! The four pigeons lay dead.

'They will make a nice pie for dinner,' said Sarah, 'and now perhaps our strawberries can ripen undisturbed!'

But she was wrong. That evening ten more

fine, fat strawberries disappeared. Theodore was nearly at his wits end.

'Only ten left!' he moaned. 'What is to be done? Am I to spend every waking moment watching from the bedroom window? What can be eating them now?'

It was a rabbit! Sarah saw it from the corner of her eye as she was tipping Grunter's food into his trough.

'Well,' she said to herself. 'We might as well have a rabbit pie,' and she sent the dog after it. The rabbit took fright and raced away across the fields but the little dog ran faster and was soon back with the rabbit in his jaws.

Theodore loved rabbit pie. He ate and ate until Sarah thought he would burst. Then he patted his stomach and laughed.

'Strawberries and cream tomorrow!' he said. 'I will go into town first thing in the morning and buy the cream. We have fought hard for these ten strawberries. I think we deserve a treat!'

True to his word he rose early next day and

went into town. He bought a large pot of best cream and a pound of softest sugar to sprinkle onto the strawberries, should they be a little sharp.

'We have ten fine, fat strawberries on our plants,' he told the grocer proudly.

'Only ten?' said the grocer, in some surprise.

'We have been very unlucky,' said Theodore. 'Ten were eaten by mice! Ten were eaten by wood-pigeons, and ten were eaten by a rabbit! We have just ten left.'

'I certainly hope you enjoy them,' said the grocer kindly. Theodore thanked him and hurried home. Sarah was waiting for him at the kitchen door, a basin in her hands.

'I thought I would wait for you,' she said, 'and then we could pick them together.'

'A very nice thought,' said Theodore.

He put the cream and sugar onto the kitchen table and together they walked down the garden. Imagine their horror when they reached the strawberry plants and saw a small fat

squirrel sitting in the middle of them as cosy as
you please. As they watched speechlessly he
nibbled his way through the last fine, fat strawberry and sprang nimbly into the safety of a
nearby tree!

# Digging for treasure

The time came for the meadow to be ploughed and sown with wheat. Sarah knew, however, that it was no good asking her husband to do it.

'That man will think of a hundred good reasons why he shouldn't do it, and not one good reason why he should,' she told herself. 'If he's to plough that field he will have to *want* to do it. Now let me think . . .'

As soon as she had finished thinking she went into town. She went first to the butcher, and asked for a pound of sausages.

'Have you heard the news?' she asked him, as he weighed the sausages. 'They say there is treasure buried in our meadow!'

'Treasure?' cried the butcher in amazement. 'Good gracious me! What sort of treasure, may I ask?'

'Golden sovereigns, so they say,' said Sarah.

'It seems that many years ago a highwayman lived in these parts and one night, after he had robbed a coach, he buried the money in our meadow, meaning to return for it the next day. But that night he was killed and the treasure has lain there to this day!'

'What a story!' cried the butcher, wrapping up the sausages. 'I suppose your husband is already busy digging up the field!'

Sarah looked very alarmed at his words and put a finger to her lips.

'Oh, please don't mention a word of this to my husband,' she begged. 'He is not a strong man and so much digging would be bad for him. No, the treasure must stay where it is. I am not a greedy woman and my husband's health means more to me than a handful of golden sovereigns.'

So saying she paid for the sausages and hurried out of the shop. She went straight along the road to the grocer.

'A pound of best butter, please,' she said, 'and a slice of cheese.'

While the grocer was cutting the cheese she asked him if he had heard the rumours.

'Rumours?' said the grocer. 'No, I have heard no rumours.'

'Well,' said Sarah. 'It seems that there is treasure buried in our meadow!'

'Treasure!' cried the grocer, forgetting all about the cheese. 'What sort of treasure, may I ask?'

'Rubies and pearls,' Sarah told him. 'It seems that many years ago a robber came this way with a jewel box he had stolen from a grand lady. The box held a ruby ring, a pearl

necklace and many other beautiful and price-less things. He meant to sell the jewels one at a time so he buried the box. To celebrate he drank a bottle of wine and then another – until he quite forgot what he was about and wandered off. Next morning he came back to look for the box but he had forgotten where it was buried. He dug and dug and dug – but he never found it. It is there still, so they say!'

'What a tale!' cried the grocer enviously. 'Now all your husband has to do is find the box of jewels and he will be a rich man. He will never need to work again.'

'Please, oh please,' said Sarah. 'Not a word of this must reach my husband. I don't want him digging away hour after hour for the sake of a few jewels. He is not a young man and might overtire himself. I trust you will not tell him.'

So saying she paid for the butter and cheese and hurried home to the farm. As soon as she had gone the grocer ran next door to tell the fishmonger. He told his wife and she told her mother and she told her sister! Meanwhile the butcher had told his story to his son. He told his aunt and she told her cousin! And so it went on! By the next morning the whole town was buzzing with rumour.

Of course, Sarah Bodgitt sent Theodore into town to buy a packet of pins, and he came home in a terrible state.

'Sarah! Sarah!' he cried. 'Everyone is saying there is treasure buried in our meadow! No less than ten people have asked me if they can dig for it! The very idea! Fetch me my big boots, woman, and a spade!'

'Theodore Bodgitt!' cried his wife sternly. 'You are not to go out into that field digging for treasure. You should know better than to listen to rumours. I'm sure there is no truth in the rumours. It is quite absurd!'

But Theodore wouldn't listen.

'Fetch me a spade, I say,' he shouted. 'The biggest one you can find. And don't bother to cook me any dinner. I shan't have time for it. I shall keep digging until I have found the money and the jewels. I shall be rich!'

'But you are not a strong man,' said Sarah. 'You have often told me so. I beg you to think again!'

'I'm as fit as a fiddle!' roared Theodore. 'I always have been. Now let me hear no more such talk from you.'

'Very well, dear,' said Sarah meekly, and she found his big boots and gave him the biggest spade she could find. Theodore ran out into the meadow and began to dig. His wife watched him for a while and then went on with her work, humming softly to herself.

Poor Theodore dug all that day and most of the evening, but he found nothing. Sarah cooked him a fine supper and rubbed liniment into his aching back.

'Why don't you use the plough, tomorrow,' she suggested slyly. 'It is old and rusty but we could oil it. It would be easier than digging.'

'Sarah, my love,' said Theodore, 'you are a clever woman. That is an excellent idea. To-morrow I will do just that!'

But the next morning Theodore woke full of aches and pains from the previous day's digging.

'Oh dear,' he wailed. 'I'm in agony! I ache all over. I can hardly lift my head from the pillow! I shan't be able to do any work today, dearest.'

'Of course you can't,' said Sarah kindly. 'You lie there and I will bring up your break-fast. But first I want to find out what those men are doing in our field. I do believe they're digging!'

Theodore sat up in bed, his face purple with

anger, his aches and pains soon forgotten.

'Digging?' he bellowed. 'Digging in my field? The audacity of it! There'll be no digging in that field that isn't done by me! Fetch me my shotgun!'

Fortunately for Sarah he didn't bother to look out of the window, for the field was as empty as a desert! He pulled on his clothes, seized the shotgun, and went roaring out into the yard.

'That's strange,' said Sarah innocently, 'they seem to have gone! Perhaps they saw you coming. But since you are already up and about, shall we oil the plough and harness the horse?'

The plough, though old and rusty, still worked well, and the horse was excited to be back in the fields again. Even Theodore began to enjoy himself. As he guided the plough the earth turned soft and brown before him, and the gulls, hungry for worms, circled the air behind him. The sun warmed his aching muscles and he began to whistle for the joy of living. Sarah watched him, smiling, from the window.

'He always could turn a straighter furrow than any man in these parts,' she said proudly, and she went into town to fetch the wheat for the next day's planting.

By nightfall the field was finished and Theodore sat down to a hearty supper with a healthy appetite and glowing cheeks.

'I'm sorry I didn't find any treasure,' he told his wife. 'Not a single sovereign! Not a solitary pearl! But do you know, I can't recall when I've enjoyed a day more!'

Sarah smiled at him wisely.

'Perhaps that is treasure enough, husband,' she said.